Escalator Escapade

Holly Smith Dinbergs

illustrated by

Chantal Stewart

RISING

...NG STARS UK LTD
22 Grafton Street, London, W1...

All rights reserved.
No part of this publication may be produced, stored in a retrieval system, or transmitted, in any form by any means, electronic, mechanical, photocopying, recording or otherwise, without the prior permission of the copyright holder.

For more information visit our website at:
www.risingstars-uk.com

British Library Cataloguing in Publication Data
A CIP record for this book is available from the British Library.

ISBN: 978-1-84680-065-8

First published in 2006 by
MACMILLAN EDUCATION AUSTRALIA PTY LTD
627 Chapel Street, South Yarra 3141

Visit our website at www.macmillan.com.au or go directly to
www.macmillanlibrary.com.au

Associated companies and representatives throughout the world.

Copyright © Holly Smith Dinbergs, Felice Arena and Phil Kettle 2006

Series created by Felice Arena and Phil Kettle
Project management by Limelight Press Pty Ltd
Cover and text design by Lore Foye
Illustrations by Chantal Stewart
Printed in China

UK Editorial by Westcote Computing Editorial Services

GIRLS ROCK!
Contents

Sophie   *Jess*

CHAPTER 1

Runaway Ring

Jess and Sophie are at the shops.
They are having a look around while
Jess's mum gets her hair done.

Jess "See you later, Mum. Don't
worry, we won't get up to mischief.
I promise!"

Sophie "Does your mum think we're going to get into trouble?"

Jess (shrugging) "Well, remember last time when we were here and we pretended to be spies?"

Sophie "Yes. That security guard went crazy."

Jess "Mmm ... he really got cross when he couldn't find us!"

Sophie "That was so funny."

Jess "Mum didn't think so. She went on about that for days."

The girls stop in front of a jewellery stall.

Jess "Ooh look! Silver rings. Cool, I love these!"

Jess tries a ring on every finger. She stretches out her fingers to admire the jewellery.

Jess "Who do I remind you of?"
Sophie "Who?"
Jess "Think 'crystal ball'."

Jess waves her hands over an imaginary crystal ball and smiles mysteriously.

Sophie "You mean the fortune-teller from the fair?"

Jess "That's right!"

Sophie "Now all you need is a scarf and some big earrings and the crowd will be lining up."

The lady working at the jewellery
stall frowns at the girls.

Sophie (whispering) "That lady looks
   really annoyed."
Jess "What's her problem?"
Sophie "I guess we're not supposed
   to touch this stuff unless we're
   going to buy it."

Jess (shrugging) "That's not fair! You have to try on shoes before you buy them. It's the same with rings."

Sophie "Hey, now that you mention it, come on. Let's go and try on shoes."

Jess "OK, great idea, Sophie. More shoes—just what you need."

Jess removes the rings, one by one, but she has trouble getting the last one off.

Jess "Oh no, this one's stuck. Help!"

Jess puts out her hand and Sophie tugs hard on the ring. No luck.

Jess "Owww."
Sophie "You want it off, don't you?"

Sophie pulls so hard that the ring flies off Jess's finger and on to the escalator. Before the girls know it, the ring is heading to the upper level of the shopping centre.

Sophie "Sorry about that. We'll get it back. Come on, Jess."

The girls race to the escalator.

CHAPTER 2

Excuse Me

The jewellery-stall lady calls the security guard, who runs over.

Sophie "Jess, quick, get on."

The girls jump onto the bottom step of the escalator, almost crashing into a man and little boy, who step on right in front of them.

Sophie "We'd better get that ring back or we're going to have to pay for it."

Jess "But it was an accident."

Sophie "I don't think she thinks so."

Jess "We've got to find that ring! Can you see it anywhere?"

Sophie "No, I can't see anything. We have to get higher up."

The girls try to move up the escalator, closer to where the ring landed, but they are blocked by the man and boy in front.

Sophie "Excuse me."
Jess (repeating) "Excuse me."

The man doesn't hear them, but the little boy turns and stares.

Sophie (whispering) "We can't wait for them to go first, Jess. We have to get that ring."

Jess "Try saying it again."

Sophie leans forward to the man in front.

Sophie (loudly) "Excuse me. We've got to get past. It's an emergency!"

The girls push past, which sends the man and the little boy flying.

Sophie "Sorry, mister!"

Jess "Sophie, do you see it? What if the ring gets sucked inside?"

Sophie stares hard at the escalator steps. She just has to find the ring.

Sophie (worried) "Everything looks so silvery. I can't make it out."
Jess "Hurry, we're almost at the top."

Sophie "I still don't see it."
Jess "There! There it is! Look!"

Jess points in front. The steps
begin to flatten out in front of Sophie.
There's not much time left.

Sophie "Yes! I see it!"

She reaches out to grab the ring.

CHAPTER 3

Mission Accomplished

Sophie sweeps up the ring in her hand just before it disappears through the slot at the top of the escalator.

Sophie "Got it!"

Jess "Phew! For a minute I thought you were going to have to pay for it."

Sophie "Me pay for it? You're the one with the humungous finger."

Jess "My finger's not big! That ring was too small, that's all."

Sophie "Thank goodness I got the ring or we'd both be in for it by now."

Jess "But it really wasn't my fault."

Sophie "Yes, yes. Come on. Let's go and give it back while we've still got it. Then we can get to the shoes."

Jess "You and your shoes. Anyone would think you owned half a shoe company the way you go on about them. I'm getting hungry. Let's go to the food court first."

Sophie "Is there ever any time when you're not hungry?"

The girls step back onto the escalator.
Sophie's shoelace is trailing behind her.

Jess "I think there's someone waiting
down there for us."

Sophie "Oh no."

Jess "What do you mean? Who is it?"

Sophie "Isn't that the same security guard who chased us around last time?"

Jess squints at the guard.

Jess "Yes, you're right. He won't be happy to see us again."

Sophie "But this was an accident. The ring was lost and we found it. We should get a reward."

Jess "Yes, right. As if that lady's going to give us a reward."

The girls approach the bottom of the escalator. As the steps start to flatten out, Sophie tries to move forward.

Sophie (shouting) "Hey, Jess! Help!"

CHAPTER 4

Seriously Stuck

Sophie tries to get Jess's attention,
She calls out again, more loudly this
time.

Sophie "Help! I'm stuck!"
Jess "What do you mean 'stuck'?"
Sophie (louder still) "I can't move my
    foot!"

Jess "What do you mean you can't move your foot?"

Sophie (upset) "Why are you repeating everything I say? Can't you see? I'm stuck. I can't move my foot!"

Jess "What's that string?"

Sophie "That's it! It's my shoelace, it's caught. I'm going to get sucked into the escalator. Help!"

Jess pulls hard on Sophie's leg
to try to release the shoelace, but it
won't loosen. Sophie becomes more
and more panicked the closer she
gets to the bottom.

Jess "Kick it off!"
Sophie "I've tried."
Jess "Well, try harder."
Sophie "I can't. It's too tight. Help!"

The security guard notices that Sophie is in trouble. He sees the caught shoelace and immediately pushes the emergency stop button.

Sophie "Phew! Thanks mister. Just in time!"

CHAPTER 5

Chips and Laces

There's a loud grinding sound as the escalator comes to a stop. The security guard gets out his pen knife and cuts the shoelace free.

Jess "Oh, Sophie, are you okay? Crikey, that was close!"

Sophie "Phew, I'll say! What would have happened if I'd been sucked into the escalator?"

Jess "I don't know. You might have been mince meat. You know, perfect for a Sophie-burger!"

Sophie "Oh, that's gross. Funny ... but gross."

Jess "At least you can give back the ring now."

Sophie looks puzzled.

Sophie "Me? But I gave it to you."
Jess "What?"
Sophie "The ring. I gave it to you."
Jess "Er … no!"

The jewellery-stall lady and the
security guard are standing together,
looking at the girls.

Jess "Sophie, I don't have it."

Sophie (laughing) "Got you! Relax. Just kidding. I have it."

Jess "You ...! Anyway, you better give it back to the lady."

Sophie "Here you are, here's your ring back. We're sorry."

The security guard opens his mouth to say something to the girls just as Jess's Mum comes out of the hairdresser.

Jess (overacting) "Mum! Your hair looks really great. Best you've ever had! Can we eat lunch now? I'm starving!"

Sophie "Sounds like a plan."

Jess "Let's eat at Burger Spot. They have really great chips there."

Jess leads her Mum towards a takeaway food place at the other end of the centre, as far away from the security guard as they can get.

Jess "I love Burger Spot. I think I'll
have a … er … a Sophie-burger … I
mean a cheeseburger!"

Sophie rolls her eyes, as Jess's
Mum asks them what they've been
up to.

Jess "Long story, Mum. But, first,
can we buy Sophie some shoelaces?
I think she needs a new pair."

GIRLS ROCK!
Escalator Lingo

Jess

Sophie

conveyor belt A flexible belt that moves things from one place to another using wheels. It moves the steps of an escalator up or down.

emergency stop button A button you push to stop the escalator—but only if there's a real emergency (like if someone gets their shoelace stuck).

escapade A wacky adventure.

handrail The thick rubber belt that you hold on to when you are on the escalator to make sure you don't fall over.

steps The moving part of the escalator that you stand on to go up or down (or where stray rings can land!).

GIRLS ROCK!

Escalator Must-dos

☆ Don't let anything drag (like super-long hair or untied shoelaces) when you ride an escalator. If it gets caught, you might turn into mince meat!

☆ Treat escalators with the same respect you'd give a bus. They are both about six tonnes of moving machinery!

☆ If you have (or see) an emergency and need to stop the escalator, shout "Stop the escalator!" in a loud voice and push the emergency stop button.

☆ Never, ever push the emergency stop button on an escalator unless it's really an emergency.

☆ Never try to walk up the "down" escalator, or down the "up" escalator. Your brain will get confused and you'll probably fall over!

☆ If you've eaten a lot of pizza or are training for a marathon, forget the escalator and use the stairs.

☆ Keep to the right if you are standing on an escalator. Then people who are in a hurry are free to walk on the left-hand side.

GIRLS ROCK!

Escalator Instant Info

The word "escalator" was made up by combining *scala*—the Latin word for steps—and the word "elevator."

Escalators are faster than elevators for short distances. You can move a lot more people quickly on escalators.

The first escalator was installed in 1897 in New York in the United States.

The world's longest escalator system (a bunch of connected escalators) is in Hong Kong. It's 800 metres long and moves 36,000 people a day.

A man from Sri Lanka set the record for walking up and down escalators in a shopping centre. He did 14,000 laps—a total of 250 kilometres—to raise money for charity.

In the London subway system (called "the Tube"), there are 409 escalators. They travel a distance equal to two round-the-world trips every week.

The longest freestanding escalator in the world is in Atlanta, Georgia, in the United States. It is about eight storeys high (50 metres).

GIRLS ROCK!
Think Tank

1 Where did the word "escalator" come from?

2 In what city of the world would you be able to have the longest ride on one escalator system?

3 Where was the first escalator installed?

4 What sort of belt helps the steps of an escalator move up or down?

5 What's the handrail on an escalator made of?

6 If you or a friend get something caught in an escalator, what should you do?

7 What were the first escalators made of?

8 How many escalators are in the London subway?

Answers

1. The word "escalator" comes from combining *scala* (the Latin word for steps) with the word "elevator".

2. You'd be able to have the longest ride on one escalator system in Hong Kong.

3. The first escalator was installed in New York.

4. A conveyor belt helps the steps of an escalator move up or down.

5. The handrail on an escalator is made of rubber (it's a giant elastic band).

6. If you or a friend get something caught in an escalator, shout "Stop the escalator, something's caught," and push the emergency stop button.

7. The first escalators were made of wood.

8. There are 409 escalators in the London subway.

How did you score?

- If you got all 8 answers correct, you're ready to study engineering and design escalators.

- If you got 6 answers correct, you can apply for a holiday job as an escalator inspector at your local shopping centre.

- If you got fewer than 4 answers correct, you'd better stay away from escalators and use the stairs!

Hey Girls!

I love to read and hope you do, too! The first book I really loved was a book called "Mary Poppins". It was full of magic (way before Harry Potter) and it got me hooked on reading. I went to the library every Saturday and left with a pile of books so heavy I could hardly carry them!

Here are some ideas about how you can make "Escalator Escapade" even more fun. At school, you and your friends can be actors and put on this story as a play. To bring the story to life, you can use props such as a silver ring, stairs for an escalator or shoes with laces trailing behind.

Who will be Sophie? Who will be Jess? Who will be the narrator? (That's the person who reads the parts between Sophie or Jess saying something.) Once you've decided on these details, you're ready to act out the story in front of the class. I bet everyone will clap when you are finished! Hey, a talent scout from a television channel might just be watching!

See if someone at home will read this story out loud with you. Reading at home is important and a lot of fun as well.

You know what my Dad used to tell me? "Readers are leaders!"

And remember, Girls Rock!

GIRLS ROCK!

Holly

When We Were Kids

Shey

Holly talked to Shey, another *Girls Rock!* author.

Shey "Did they have escalators when you were little?"

Holly "Very funny. I'm not that old!"

Shey "Just kidding. Did you ever have a problem with an escalator?"

Holly "Not me, but my best friend did. We were chatting and her shoelace really did get caught."

Shey "Was she OK?"

Holly "Yes. Her Dad pulled really hard, and her shoelace broke."

Shey "Does she still have the shoes?"

Holly "No, now she only wears shoes without laces!"

GIRLS ROCK!
What a Laugh!

Q Why did the ghost go up the escalator?

A To raise its spirits.

GIRLS ROCK!

The Sleepover

Pool Pals

Bowling Buddies

Girl Pirates

Netball Showdown

School Play Stars

Diary Disaster

Horsing Around

Newspaper Scoop

Snowball Attack

Dog on the Loose

Escalator Escapade

Cooking Catastrophe

Talent Quest

Wild Ride

Camping Chaos

Mummy Mania

Skater Chicks

GIRLS ROCK! books are available from most booksellers. For mail order information please call Rising Stars on 0870 40 20 40 8 or visit www.risingstars-uk.com

44